THIS IS THE TRUE STORY

of an injured sea turtle found on a Florida beach, told from the turtle's point of view.*

~ ~ ~ ~ ~ ~ ~ ~   DEDICATION   ~ ~ ~ ~ ~ ·

For my students — who like Mahi — faced challenges, persisted, and triumphed.
SUZANNE JACOBS LIPSHAW

For Lola. For Jim & Mary P. You are rescuers. You are lovers. Stay strong!
DOROTHY SHAW

~ ~ ~

*See page 30 for more details.

Simple activities designed to help parents and/or caregivers participate in, and support, a child's literacy skills and educational goals:

Linking to Literacy

- **Easiest**: Mighty and Mahi begin with the letter Mm. As you read the story together, see how many Mms you can find.

- More Difficult: Watch for these common sight words that contain the letter Mm: my, me, am, must. There are more words that contain the letter Mm. Can you find them?

- Challenging: Look at this picture of a sea turtle. Can you find its flippers, shell, eyes, and mouth? There are lots of fun facts about sea turtles at the back of this book!

*For free, printable resources, visit **www.doodleandpeck.com**, and click on the Linking to Literacy **tab**.

I am a green sea turtle.

I travel the ocean, gliding through the salty current.
My front flippers propel me through the
waves like wings. My back flippers
steer me like a rudder on a boat.
I nibble on seagrass,

MIGHTY MAHI

By Suzanne Jacobs Lipshaw

Illustrated by Dorothy Shaw

ISBN 978-1-7358306-5-0 (paperback)
ISBN 978-1-7358306-6-7 (hard cover)

Doodle and Peck Publishing
413 Cedarburg Ct
Yukon, OK 73099
405.354.7422
www.doodleandpeck.com

Temporary cataloging topics:
Easy/Sea turtles/acquarium/ocean life/picture book/veterinarian/ages 3-8/grades PK-3
Description: A green sea turtle is injured by trash in the ocean. Veterinarians at a nearby
sea aquarium must come to his rescue.

Library of Congress Control Number: 2021942859

I swim to the
surface to take
a breath,
then in a flash,
I dive back
into the sea.

I see something

shiny ahead. It

sparkles

under the sun.

I swim over to take a look.

Uh oh!

The stringy thing is caught on my flipper.

I tug,
I pull,
and
I yank.

Still,
it won't
come loose.

But I am STRONG.

I swim on.
Maybe it will fall off.

Instead, it tightens
around my flipper.

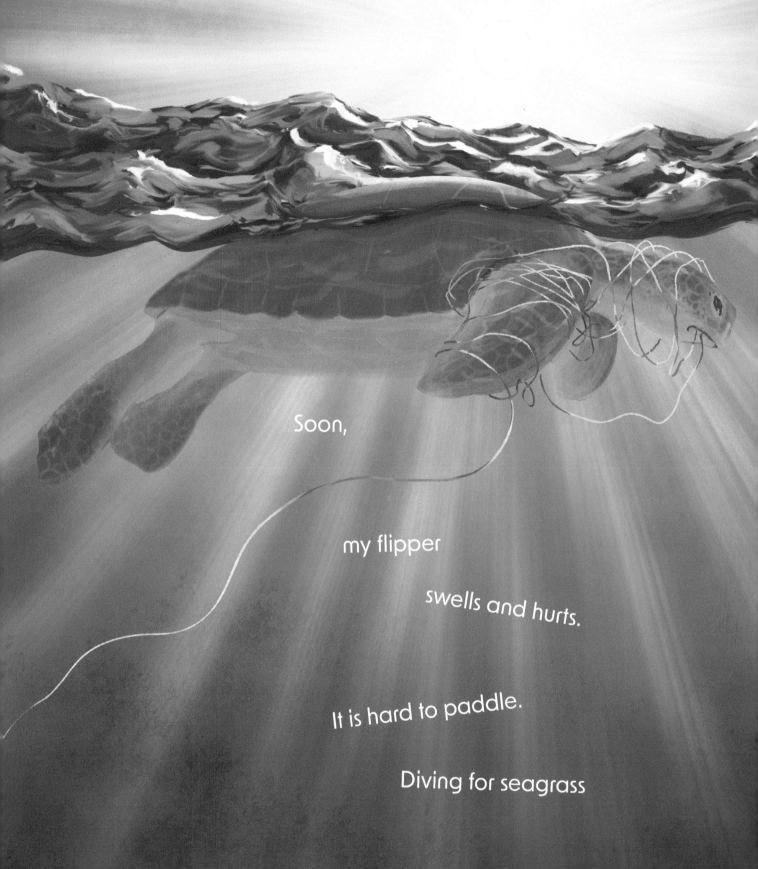

Soon,

my flipper

swells and hurts.

It is hard to paddle.

Diving for seagrass

is impossible.

12

Tired, I ride the surf and wash up onto the shore.

I drag myself
further onto land.

OH NO!

Something is in my way! I zig and zag,
but it's useless. I am trapped!
Hungry and tired, I lay still.

Then,

HOORAY!

A human cuts
the stringy
thing.
I'm free!
Another
human
takes me
to a place
where they
examine me.

They look at my flipper.
It's in bad shape and
needs to be removed.
They worry I
may not
survive.

But I am STRONG.

I am so strong, the people at the
rescue center call me Mahi.
Mahi is the Hawaiian word
for very strong. Only five
days after surgery, I am
strong enough to swim
in a shallow tank.

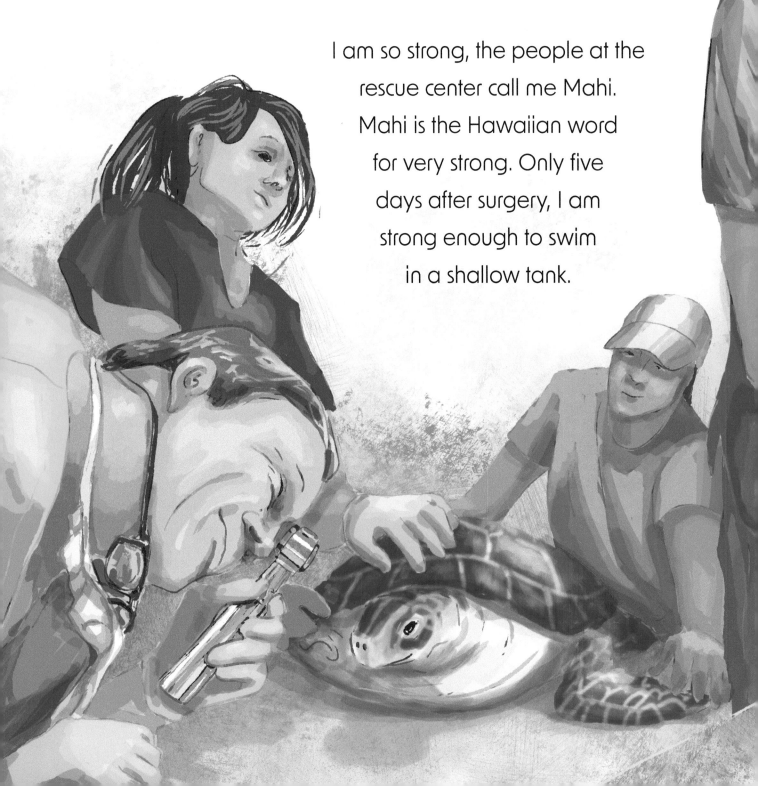

Still,
I am not
allowed to
go home.

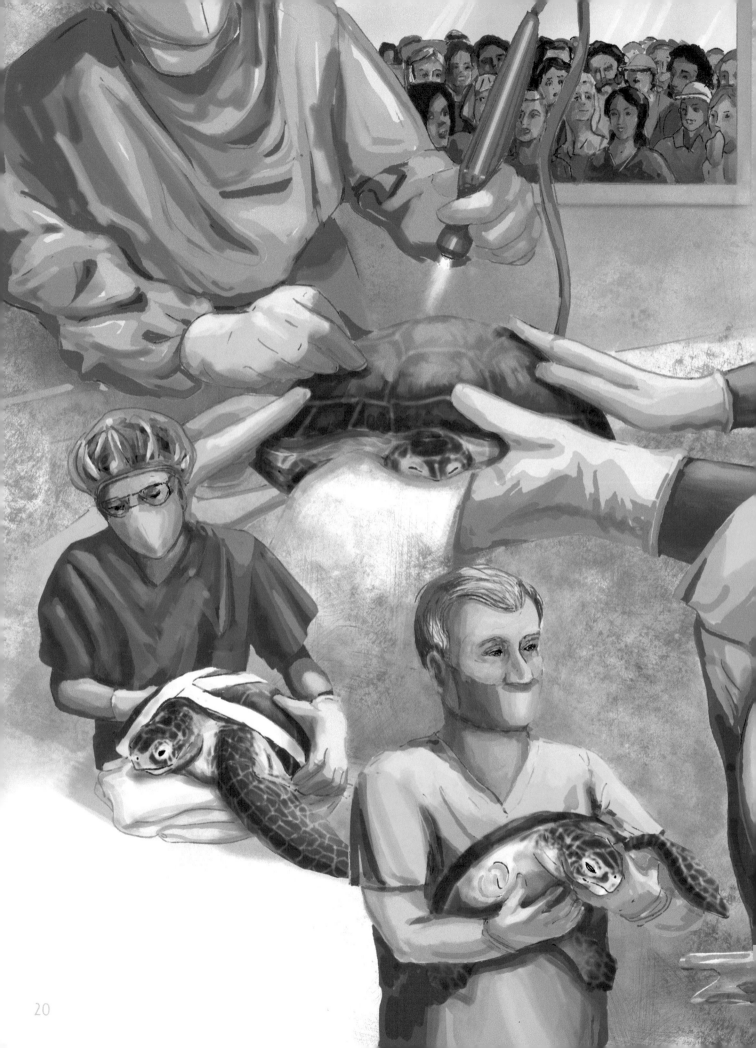

Even with special care, my wound doesn't heal. My treatments are so expensive that the center finds 1,200 sea turtle lovers to help pay for my care. I have more adoptive parents than any turtle has ever had at the Georgia Sea Turtle Center!

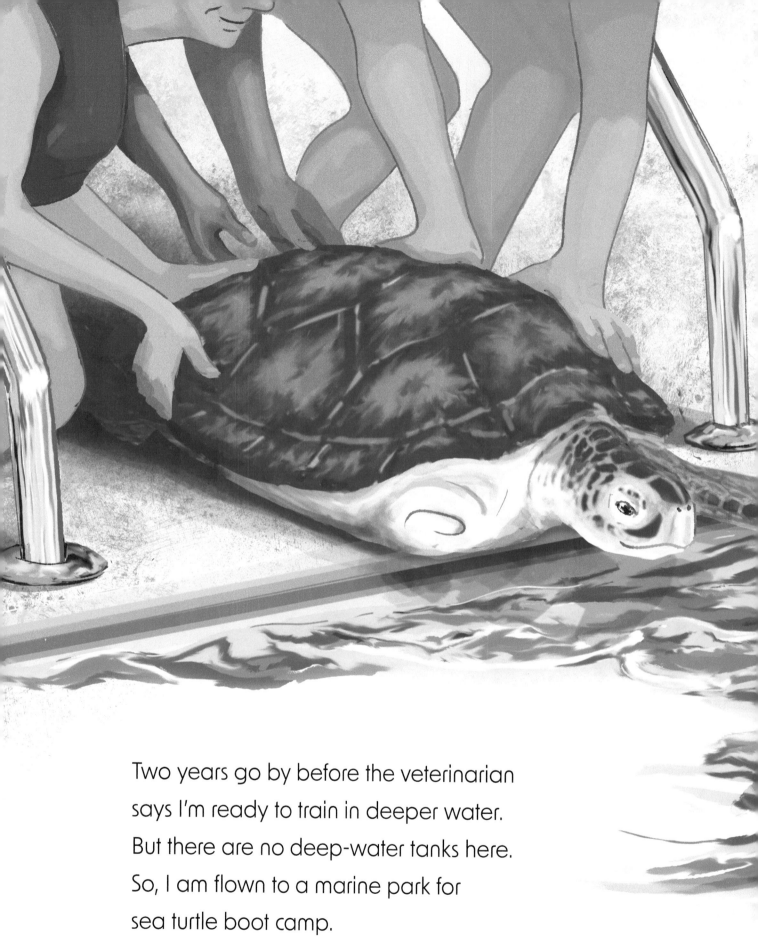

Two years go by before the veterinarian
says I'm ready to train in deeper water.
But there are no deep-water tanks here.
So, I am flown to a marine park for
sea turtle boot camp.

In their giant tanks,
I must relearn to
swim, dive, and feed.

But I am STRONG.

I learn all these things —
with only **three** flippers.
I can finally go home.

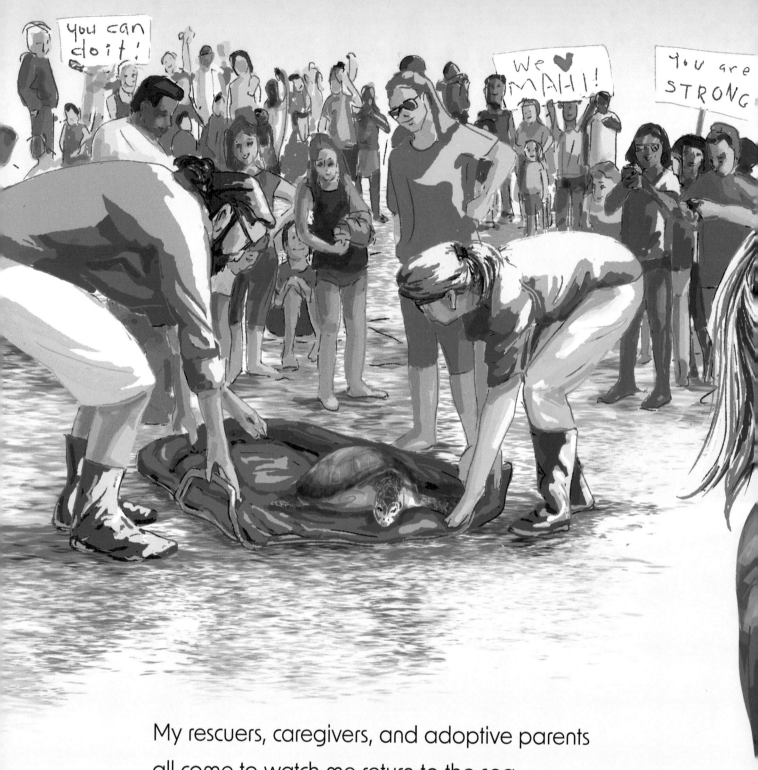

My rescuers, caregivers, and adoptive parents
all come to watch me return to the sea.

A human carries me to the edge of the
ocean and pushes me out into the sea.
The waves splash my face and shell.

Soon I am gliding
through the salty current.
My mighty front flipper propels
me through the waves.
My back flippers
steer me further
into the ocean.

I nibble on seagrass, then swim to the ocean surface to take a breath.

I AM MAHI!
Very strong
indeed.

In a flash, I dive deep into the sea.

Sea Turtle Trivia

1. There are **SEVEN SPECIES** of sea turtles: green, loggerhead, leatherback, hawksbill, kemps ridley, flatback, and olive ridley — all are endangered.

2. Sea turtles have been around as long as **DINOSAURS**. They have explored the oceans for over 100 million years.

3. Sea turtles are **REPTILES**. Like all reptiles, they are cold-blooded, have a three-chambered heart, and scaly skin.

4. Sea turtles are related to land turtles but have **FLIPPERS** instead of legs.

5. Unlike other turtles, sea turtles **CANNOT** bring their legs and head into their shells for protection.

6. Sea turtles can be yellow, greenish, and black depending on the species. Green sea turtles are not green on the outside. They are called green sea turtles because of the **GREEN LAYER OF FAT** they have under their shell. Scientists believe the green fat comes from all the plants they eat.

7. Some sea turtles are **ENORMOUS**. The largest leatherback ever recorded weighed 2,019 pounds and measured almost ten feet.

8. The sea turtle's shell is called a **CARAPACE**. It is made out of bone and cartilage. All sea turtles, except for leatherbacks, have thin plates on their carapace called **SCUTES**. You can tell what species a sea turtle is by looking at its color, carapace, and the number and pattern of its scutes.

9. Sea turtles can be **CARNIVORES, HERBIVORES, OR OMNIVORES**. Some of their favorite foods are jellyfish, seaweed, shrimp, crabs, snails, sponges, algae, and mollusks.

10. Sea turtles **TRAVEL** very long distances. A leatherback sea turtle can swim more than 10,000 miles every year.

11. Sea turtles **HOLD THEIR BREATH** for a long time. Most can hold their breath for more than thirty minutes. Green sea turtles can stay underwater for as long as five hours.

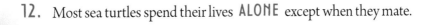

12. Most sea turtles spend their lives ALONE except when they mate.

13. When it is time for female sea turtles to give birth, they lay their eggs on land in a nest called a CLUTCH. They return to the same nesting grounds where they were born. They lay between 50 – 200 eggs. Sea turtle eggs look like PING PONG BALLS.

14. Baby sea turtles are called HATCHLINGS. Hatchlings use the light of the moon to guide them from their clutch across the sandy beach to begin their life in the ocean.

15. Unfortunately, only one out of one thousand hatchlings will survive and become an adult sea turtle. If they make it to adulthood, sea turtles can live as long as 150 YEARS.

16. The GENDER of a sea turtle is determined by how hot or cold the sand is around their nest. Warmer temperatures produce more female hatchlings and cooler temperatures produce more males.

17. You cannot tell if a sea turtle is a BOY OR GIRL when it is born. You have to wait approximately 30 years and then look at the size of its tail. If the tail is thick and extends past its hind flippers, it is male. If the tail is thinner and shorter, it is a female.

18. SEA TURTLES CRY, but not because they are sad. They have glands in their eyes that produce tears. The tears wash away excess salt from their eyes.

19. THE BIGGEST THREATS to sea turtles are fishing gear, artificial lights, water pollution, global warming, natural predators, and human predators.

20. WE CAN PROTECT SEA TURTLES by throwing away all our garbage when visiting a beach, limiting single-use plastics, putting away our chairs and umbrellas from the beach at night, and only buying fish that has been caught by fishermen who use turtle-friendly methods.

Photos of Mahi courtesy of the Jekyll Island Authority's Georgia Sea Turtle Center

More About MAHI

Mahi was found in Florida on January 14, 2013, by a hiker who contacted a park ranger to free Mahi. The ranger called the Florida Fish and Wildlife Commission and they arranged for Mahi's transfer to the Georgia Sea Turtle Center. When Mahi arrived at the center, she was in critical condition. Along with having fishing line wrapped around her flipper, Mahi had swallowed some of the line. It was caught in her throat and went down into her stomach. The center's veterinarian, Dr. Terry Norton, performed emergency surgery to remove the swallowed line. Her flipper was amputated the next day.

Mahi had multiple surgeries throughout her stay at the center along with specialized laser treatments. Before Mahi left, her caregivers inserted a Passive Integrative Transponder (PIT tag) into her. A PIT tag is a unique number/letter sequence

that will identify Mahi if she is found after being released into the ocean. The staff chose not to track Mahi because they were concerned the addition of a satellite transmitter would make swimming and diving more difficult for a turtle with only three flippers. Mahi's was released on July 7, 2015, at Vilano Beach in St. Augustine, Florida — very close to where she was found. Over 200 supporters cheered Mahi on as she swam back into the sea.

BIBLIOGRAPHY

Bradford, Alina. "Facts About Sea Turtles." *Livescience.com*. N.p., 21 July 2016. Web. 20 Apr. 2018.

Center, Georgia Sea Turtle. "Happy 10th! Georgia Sea Turtle Center Celebrating Decade of Progress in Conservation, Research and Animal Welfare." *PR Newswire: News Distribution, Targeting and Monitoring*. PRNewswire, 09 June 2017. Web. 20 Apr. 2018.

"Georgia Sea Turtle Center." *Jekyll Island Georgia*. N.p., n.d. Web. 01 Mar. 2018.

"Green Sea Turtle Facts for Kids." *National Geographic Kids*. N.p., 01 May 2017. Web. 20 Apr. 2018.

"Gulf World Marine Institute – Dedicated to Sea Turtle and Marine Mammal Rescue, Rehabilitation, and Release." *Gulf World Marine Institute*. N.p., n.d. Web. 20 Apr. 2018.

Kearns, Landess. "12 Sea Turtle Facts That Prove How Cool They Are." *The Huffington Post*. TheHuffingtonPost.com, 07 Dec. 2017. Web. 20 Apr. 2018.

Kennedy, Jennifer. "10 Fun Facts About Sea Turtles." *ThoughtCo*. ThoughtCo, 20 June 2017. Web. 20 Apr. 2018.

"Mahi the Sea Turtle Is Finally Home." *Home*. N.p., 08 July 2015. Web. 20 Apr. 2018.

"Nancy Condron - Whitney Lab for Marine Bioscience (Drove Mahi to the GSTC)." Telephone interview. 1 May 2018.

Ratika. "25 Fun Facts About Sea Turtle for Kids." *MomJunction*. Incnut Incnut, 10 Mar. 2017. Web. 20 Apr. 2018.

"Sea Turtle Conservancy – Helping *Sea Turtles Survive Since 1959*." *Sea Turtle Conservancy*. N.p., n.d. Web. 20 Apr. 2018.

Stearns, Kira. "Georgia Sea Turtle Center Mahi Adoption Update." Email distribution. *Mahi Adoption Update*. Georgia Sea Turtle Center, n.d. Web. 9 May 2018.

Helping Hands

The Georgia Sea Turtle Center

The Georgia Sea Turtle Center (GSTC) is a hospital and rehabilitation center dedicated to helping injured turtles and increasing awareness about sea turtles through education, conservation, and research. It has an interactive exhibit gallery and rehabilitation pavilion where visitors can come to see and learn about the sea turtle patients. When a turtle is brought to

Photos courtesy of the Jekyll Island Authority's Georgia Sea Turtle Center

the GSTC it is examined by a veterinarian. A center technician weighs the turtle, checks its blood cell count, and removes any debris stuck to the turtle's shell. The turtles stay at the center while they are treated. Those, like Mahi, who are healthy and independent are released back into the ocean. Those that can't return to the sea, are flown to a zoo or an aquarium. For more information or to make a donation, please visit their website at www.georgiaseaturtlecenter.org.

Gulf World Marine Institute

The Gulf World Marine Institute is the marine park Mahi went to for sea turtle boot camp. It is dedicated to sea turtle and mammal rescue, rehabilitation, and release. The facility provides short- and long-term care to marine animals. The Gulf World Marine Park is open to visitors who want to learn about and interact with sea turtles and other marine animals. For more information or to make a donation, please visit their website at www.gulfworldmarinepark.com.

Mrs. Lipshaw's Lore

(Author's Note from a Teacher)

During the 2014-15 school year, my elementary reading students boarded an imaginary yellow submarine from Northville, Michigan to Jekyll Island, Georgia for a virtual field trip to the Georgia Sea Turtle Center (GSTC). Our tour guide, Kira, taught us about sea turtles and how those found sick

© *John Heider – USA TODAY NETWORK*

or injured are cared for in the center's hospital. One of the first turtle patients we met was a juvenile green sea turtle who was missing her right front flipper — Mahi!

On our tour, we also learned about the dangers sea turtles face because of human disregard. This was when Kira helped me carry out my secret mission — to inspire my students to advocate for and help these endangered creatures. Kira explained that Mahi's care was expensive. To help with the costs, people could symbolically adopt her for fifty dollars. Without hesitation one of my students jumped out of his chair, pumped his fist into the air, and shouted "Yes, we can do that!"

We formulated a plan to raise money to adopt Mahi starting with informing our school community about the threats sea turtles face. Students presented a taped "virtual assembly" focusing on what we, even in Michigan, could do to protect sea turtles. Then, they sold reusable collapsible water bottles for donation — raising over $1,700. As one student said, "We feel good about what we've learned so far and what we've been able to do. We feel a lot of pride in helping the turtles."

MISSION ACCOMPLISHED!

SUZANNE JACOBS LIPSHAW

Suzanne Jacobs Lipshaw is a children's book author and former special education teacher who is passionate about growing young minds. Suzanne enjoys speaking to schools about writing, leadership, and how kids can make a difference in our world. The proud momma of two grown boys, Suzanne lives in Waterford, Michigan with her husband and furry writing companion, Ziggy. When she's not dreaming up new writing projects, you can find her kayaking on the lake, hiking the trail, practicing at the yoga studio, or dabbling in interior design.

To learn more about Suzanne, please visit her website at:
www.suzannejacobslipshaw.com

DOROTHY SHAW

Dorothy is a designer, illustrator, painter, sculptor, mom, and grandmother. As a visual communicator, her goal is to explode and organize information into new dimensions of understanding and experiences. She loves color, and she loves books. "Read!" she says, and "Read to the children in your life!" Look for other childen's books that she has written and/or illustrated, including *Jerome the Stone, Kate's Ocean, Suki and Sam, Joshua and the Biggest Fish*, and *Camp Not Allowed.*

To learn more about Dorothy, please visit her website at:
www.dorothyshaw.com

MAHI

Mahi was born in the wild. Swimming the ocean with carefree abandon, she was entangled by human debris. Fortunately, she was also rescued by a human. After her harrowing experience, she was rehabilitated and released back into the wild, to swim strong and free once again.

To watch a video about Mahi and learn more about sea turtle rescues, please go to:
https://fb.watch/6Npe0thm6x/

Courtesy of the Jekyll Island Authority's Georgia Sea Turtle Center